ISBN   0 904494 74 8
© BRIMAX RIGHTS LTD. 1978
PUBL. BY BRIMAX BOOKS 1980
FIRST PUBLISHED IN 1978
BY BRIMAX BOOKS UNDER THE TITLE OF
ADVENTURES AT ASH LODGE - EXPLORING

WOODLAND MISCHIEF

WOODLAND MISCHIEF

by Lucy Kincaid

Illustrated by Eric Kincaid

CONTENTS

BRIMAX BOOKS • CAMBRIDGE • ENGLAND

A MISTY MORNING

It was a cold morning. The sky seemed to have closed
in over the roof of Ash Lodge and bands of mist were curling
slowly through the trees like wisps of smoke. The birds had
stopped singing and were huddled together trying to keep warm.
Willie opened the door of Ash Lodge and shivered. He had a

letter he wanted to post in the box at the end of the lane.

"Don't be long," called Basil as Willie plodded off
into the mist. "It's getting thicker."

"I suppose you think I'll get lost," sniffed Willie.

"Just hurry, that's all," called Basil.

Willie muttered to himself crossly. "Hurry up indeed. I'll hurry as much as I want to . . . and that's not at all." And he didn't. He dragged his feet AND dawdled AND stopped AND looked inside curled-up leaves AND turned over interesting looking stones. He sat on a fallen log and took his letter from its envelope and checked that he had made no spelling mistakes. That took a nice long time because he had to have a good long think about EVERY separate word.

"I think there's only one 't' in little," he said aloud as he put the letter back into its envelope.

"That's where you're wrong, there are two," said a squirrel who was sitting on a branch just above his head.

"What do YOU know about spelling?" scoffed Willie.

"More than you do it seems," laughed the squirrel. "You've spelt socks wrong too."

"You've been reading over my shoulder," shouted Willie angrily. The squirrel laughed and dropped a nut on Willie's head.

"Ouch!" said Willie as it bounced off. "Just you wait." But before he could throw one back, the squirrel had vanished into a soft white cloud. He had vanished FAR too quickly. Startled, Willie looked round. The tops of the trees were wrapped in thick cotton wool blankets. The mist WAS getting thicker. It had crept stealthily and quietly through the trees while he wasn't looking. Perhaps Basil was right after all. Perhaps he had better hurry. He ran to the mail box as fast as his legs would take him, posted his letter and began the journey back.

The mist was getting much, much thicker. His own breath was puffing out in great white clouds. He wished his legs were longer and he could run faster. He couldn't see the edge of the path at all. Trees kept jumping out at him. Invisible twigs and branches kept catching hold of him. He was scared.

THUMP! BUMP! Suddenly he saw a hundred stars shining through the mist. He had run straight into a tree. A shower of nuts fell all around him.

"What do you think you're doing?" shouted an angry voice. "Put those nuts back, at once."

Willie didn't see the nuts
or hear the voice. He was
staggering round and round in
circles. He wished he knew
which way to go. He stumbled
on and on, getting more and
more frightened. WHERE HAD
ALL THE TREES GONE?
THUMP! BUMP! STUMBLE!

13

He was so thankful to find a tree, any tree at all, that
he didn't notice the stars dancing in front of his eyes.
He flung his arms round its smooth silky trunk and held onto
it tightly. He came to a quick decision. He was NOT
going to move another inch.

"BASIL!" he shouted as loudly as he could. "DEWY!"

"There's no need to shout," said Basil's voice from
somewhere not too far away.

"Where are you?" demanded Willie. "Where am I?"

"We're over here," called Basil. And when Willie
stared hard enough into the mist he not only saw the anxious
faces of Basil and Dewy peering back at him, he also saw his
own front door. He took a closer look at the tree he was
clasping so tightly. It wasn't a tree at all. It was one

of the smooth pillars that
supported his own porch. He
was HOME! He was SAFE! He
stumbled towards the door and
fell into the house with a
glad sigh.

"You've been gone a long
time," said Dewy. "We were
getting worried. What kept
you? Did you get lost?"

"Who? Me?" said Willie
as soon as the door was safely
shut behind him. "Of course
I didn't. I'm home aren't I?"

SOMETHING PRICKLY

In the wood the chestnuts were ripening and falling from the trees. Their prickly cases were everywhere.

"Ouch!" said Basil and hopped about on one foot.

"Why don't you look where you're putting your feet," said Willie and then trod on a spiky nutcase himself.

"OUCH!" he said, twice as loudly as Basil.

"Why don't YOU look where YOU are putting YOUR feet," said Basil and Dewy together.

"I suppose you think that's funny," said Willie.

"It is funny," said Basil, carefully avoiding another of the spiky balls.

"What's inside them anyway?" asked Willie.

"Nuts," said Dewy.

"Don't be rude," said Willie. "I asked a perfectly civil question."

"And I gave you a perfectly civil answer," said Dewy "Nuts . . ."

Willie glowered and puffed out his chest. He looked as though he might explode.

"I'll show you," said Dewy quickly. He picked up a spiky ball that had a split in its coat and prised it open.

He showed Willie the smooth brown nut that had been tucked tightly inside the spiky husk.

"They are very good to eat," he said. He peeled off the brown skin and popped the milky-white nut into his mouth.

"I would like to try one of those," said Willie.

"Then you'd better peel one, hadn't you," laughed Dewy.

"I suppose you think I can't do it," said Willie and began to juggle with a ball that seemed to be made from a million jabbing spikes.

"Ouch! Oh . . . ouch!" he winced.

While Willie juggled and got crosser and crosser but more and more determined not to be beaten, Basil and Dewy gathered a hatful of nuts to take home. At long last, Willie got the nut out of its prickly case. It was very, very tiny and his paws were very, very sore.

"Do you mean to tell me I've gone to ALL that trouble just to get THAT out?" he said crossly. He peeled off the brown skin and put the nut in his mouth. It was gone in one gulp. "They're just not worth the bother," he said.

He was trailing along behind Basil and Dewy, muttering and grumbling to himself when he caught sight of something out of the corner of his eye. He looked quickly at Basil and Dewy. THEY hadn't noticed. He suddenly found something interesting to stop and look at, then as soon as Basil and Dewy were a safe distance ahead, he scrambled into the leaves and stared with delight at the big, brown prickly ball. It was HUGE. It was GIGANTIC! A prickly something of that size would be worth peeling.

"Ouch . . . oh . . . ouch . . ." he said softly under his breath, as he picked it up and cradled it in his arms. Its prickles were incredibly sharp, but what did that matter? Just think of the size of the nut inside!

He kept his distance behind Dewy and Basil all the way home.

"I'd just like to see their faces when I'm eating this," he said. "But they won't see me because I'll eat it in secret . . ." The prickly ball got heavier and heavier. His tummy began to feel like a pin cushion.

"Where's Willie?" asked Basil when he and Dewy got home.

"He's coming," said Dewy. "I say, he seems to have found something. I wonder what it is?"

"What have you got there?" asked Basil as Willie came round the corner by the shed. Willie was taken completely by surprise. By his reckoning Basil and Dewy should have been safely indoors.

"Where? What? Oh, you mean this," he said, trying to sound casual and unconcerned. He supposed he'd have to share it with them now. "It's a chestnut."

Basil and Dewy stared at him.

"No it isn't," said Dewy.

Willie couldn't argue while he was feeling like a pin cushion, so he put the nut down. And there, right in front of him, it . . . uncurled itself . . . and RAN AWAY . . .

"Come back!" shouted Willie. "Where do you think you're going?"

"Back to his mother I shouldn't wonder," said Dewy.

"His mother?" Willie didn't understand.

"Don't you know a young hedgehog when you see one?" laughed Basil.

19

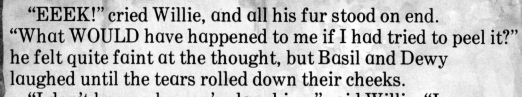

"EEEK!" cried Willie, and all his fur stood on end. "What WOULD have happened to me if I had tried to peel it?" he felt quite faint at the thought, but Basil and Dewy laughed until the tears rolled down their cheeks.

"I don't know why you're laughing," said Willie. "I don't think it's funny at all."

SMOKE

Willie was sitting in his tree house with one eye closed and one eye open. He was looking through his telescope. He could see right over the roof of Ash Lodge and to the wood beyond. There was a wisp of blue smoke curling lazily above the trees.

"See anything interesting?" called Basil from the foot of the tree house ladder.

"Just a wisp of smoke," answered Willie.

"Smoke!" gasped Basil as though seeing smoke was important. He raced up the ladder two steps at a time.

"Show me where." Basil didn't need the telescope. He could see the smoke curling up above the trees without it.

"That needs investigating," said Basil. "Where there is smoke there is bound to be fire."

"Er . . . I'll stay here and keep watch through my telescope . . . er . . . in case it gets worse . . ." said Willie nervously.

"You'll come with me," said Basil firmly. "I may need your help."

"Can't Dewy go with you instead of me," puffed Willie as he tried to keep up with Basil. Basil could move very fast when he was worried. And he was certainly worried now.

"Dewy's coming too," said Basil. "If the wood is alight we'll need all the help we can get."

Dewy didn't make excuses. He came straight away.

"How do we know where to go?" asked Willie. "We can't see the smoke from down here."

"East," said Basil. Basil had a good sense of direction. If Basil said east then east it was. He led them along the winding paths and turned left and right without a moments hesitation as though he had a map drawn inside his head.

"He'll get us lost, I know he will," whispered Willie.

Suddenly Basil stopped, and sniffed . . .

"There . . . I knew it . . . I knew it . . ." moaned Willie. "I knew I shouldn't have come . . . we're lost."

"What's that I can smell?" asked Basil, completely ignoring Willie's outburst.

"Smoke," said Dewy.

"Yes . . ." said Basil. "But there's something else . . ."

"Sausages . . ." said Dewy, rather surprisingly.

"It must be a camper." Basil gave a sigh of relief.

"Do you mean there isn't a fire to put out . . ." said Willie, ". . . and the wood isn't going to burn down?"

"I shouldn't think so," said Basil.

"Can we go home then?" asked Willie.

"Not yet," said Basil. "We must make sure."

The smell of cooking sausages got stronger. The

crackle of burning twigs became louder. Presently they came to a clearing.

"There's someone sitting there," gasped Willie and tried to turn back the way they had come.

"Sausages don't cook themselves, you know," whispered Basil keeping a firm hold on Willie.

A wily old fox was sitting in front of a campfire cooking sausages in a frying pan.

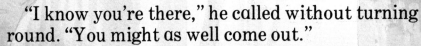

"I know you're there," he called without turning
round. "You might as well come out."

"H . . . how did he know?" whispered Willie as they all
stepped into the clearing.

"I heard you whispering," said the fox.

He gave the frying pan a good shake. "Done . . ." he said. "Excuse me while I eat . . . haven't had any breakfast yet."

"Could I . . . ?" began Willie. He couldn't help licking his lips.

"Shush," said Dewy. "Of course you can't . . ."

"Yes he can," said the fox. "You can all have a sausage if you want one, but you'll have to use sticks as forks. I've only got one."

While they all nibbled at the hot sausages which were delicately flavoured by the wood smoke, the fox told them he was a traveller and only passing through that way.

"Never stay anywhere for long," he said. "I like to travel . . . a night here . . . a night there . . . it suits me."

"Where do you sleep?" asked Willie.

The fox pointed to a rolled-up sleeping bag.

"That's all the bed I need," he said. "I sleep under the stars."

"Wouldn't suit me," said Willie.

"Don't suppose it would," said the fox. "But then you're not a fox are you?"

And though they invited him, the fox wouldn't even stay one night at Ash Lodge.

"The sky is my roof," he said. "That's the way I like it and that's the way I'm going to keep it." And nothing they said would make him change his mind.

RUN WILLIE, RUN

Basil had made a walking stick from a piece of gnarled and knobbly wood.

"Do you think I could have it?" asked Willie wistfully. "I've always wanted a walking stick like that."

"Of course you can," said Basil.

Willie was so pleased.

"What are you going to do with it now you've got it?" asked Dewy.

"Go walking with it, of course," said Willie. And he went off into the wood swinging the stick backwards and forwards, trying to keep his feet in step with it as he went. It wasn't as easy as he thought it was going to be. It took a lot of practice to get it right. He found the stick was very good at swishing aside the undergrowth and at holding prickly stems away from his legs. It was also a very good prodder and poker.

"I didn't know a walking stick had so many uses," he said as he pushed it down a hole and twiddled it about. "It's just like having an extra arm." He found another hole to prod and poke.

"Ow!" cried a voice, from somewhere underground.

"Oh dear," said Willie
and tried to pull his stick
from the hole. HE COULDN'T.
Something . . . or someone, was
holding onto the other end.
Suddenly the stick was snatched
from his grasp and something . . .
or someone . . . began to shake it
at HIM.

"EEEK!" cried Willie.

"I'll teach you to poke
sticks down burrows!" shouted
an angry voice, and before
Willie knew what was happening,
he was being chased by an angry
rabbit who was daring to shake
Willie's own stick at Willie
himself.

"Just you wait until I
catch you!" shouted the rabbit.

29

"Help!" shouted Willie. "HELP!"

"Sounds as though Willie's in trouble," said Basil.

"It looks like it too," said Dewy as Willie's roly-poly figure hurtled from the wood with the rabbit in close pursuit.

"I've never seen Willie move so quickly," said Basil. "I wonder what's up."

"Save me! SAVE ME!" shouted Willie.

"Just you wait until I catch you!" shouted the rabbit.

"That rabbit looks angry about something," said Dewy.

It was a very exciting chase to watch.

"I didn't know Willie was so good at dodging out of the way," said Basil.

"I suppose we ought to do something before he gets caught," said Dewy.

"I suppose we should," said Basil and stepped between Willie and the angry rabbit. The rabbit collided with Basil and stopped, very suddenly.

"I don't know why he's chasing me," said Willie hiding behind Basil's broad back. "I haven't done anything."

"Haven't DONE anything!" exploded the rabbit. "Look at that . . . take a look at THAT!" He parted the fur on top of his head and showed them a bump the size of a wren's egg.

"Did Willie do that?" gasped Basil.

"Willie . . ." gasped Dewy. "How could you?"

"I'll tell you how he could," said the rabbit. "He poked this stick down my burrow . . . there I was, sitting in my own armchair, minding my own business, when I was hit on the head with THIS!" He shook the stick angrily.

"You shouldn't do things like that Willie," said Basil reproachfully. "You must apologize at once."

Willie knew he must.

"I'm most terribly sorry . . ." he said. "Really I am."

Basil and Dewy took the rabbit indoors and bathed his bump with cold water. As the swelling went down the rabbit's anger subsided too.

"Ask him if I can have my walking stick back," whispered Willie in Basil's ear.

"I think you should ask him yourself," said Basil.

The rabbit gave Willie back his stick but he made him promise never to poke it down another burrow.

"Don't worry," said Willie. "I wouldn't dare. You might catch me next time."

HELPING OUT

"Come in and stay for supper," said Basil one evening, when Owl was passing the house.

"Don't mind if I do," yawned Owl and wiped his feet on the doormat.

"My, you do look tired," said Dewy.

All through supper, Owl's eyelids kept drooping.
"Would you like some more pie?" asked Dewy.
"Yes please . . ." yawned Owl and held out his plate.
"You can put it down now," said Willie. But Owl didn't
hear him . . . his eyes had finally closed . . . he was fast asleep.

"What are we going to do?" whispered Dewy as he gently took the plate from Owl and put it back on the table.

"Put him to bed," said Willie. "That's where I go when I'm tired."

"I thought Owl slept during the day and went about his business at night," said Dewy.

"So he does," said Basil.

"Why is he asleep now then?" asked Willie.

"Perhaps he's not feeling well," said Dewy.

They sat round the table discussing Owl's unusual behaviour while Owl sat with his head on his chest gently snoring and taking no part in the conversation at all.

"Why don't we wake him up and ask him?" said Willie.

"We can't do that," said Dewy.

"There might be something important he's supposed to be doing," said Willie.

"That's true," said Basil and shook Owl gently.

"Er . . . er . . . wha . . . wh . . ." Owl jerked up his head and opened his eyes. "Wh . . . where am I?"

"At Ash Lodge," said Basil. "Are you feeling alright Owl?"

34

"Not really," said Owl. His eyes closed and his head sank back onto his chest.

"What's the matter old friend?" said Basil gently.

"Got myself mixed up . . ." mumbled Owl. "Got the days and nights mixed up . . . sleep when I should be awake . . . awake when I should be asleep . . . can't seem to help it . . . getting behind with my work . . . know I'd be alright if I could stay awake just one night . . . can't seem to manage it . . ."

"Isn't there any medicine you could take?" asked Basil.

"Wish there waszzzzzzzzz . . ." sighed Owl and lapsed into another snore.

Dewy was looking thoughtful. "I'm sure we could do it if we tried," he said.

"Do what?" asked Willie.

"Keep Owl awake all night," said Dewy.

"How can we? We will be asleep ourselves," said Willie.

"We will have to stay awake," said Dewy.

"What . . . ALL night?" Willie wondered if his ears were playing tricks. But they weren't. Dewy had a plan and Willie was part of the plan whether he liked it or not.

Everywhere Owl went that night, they went too. Basil
carried a torch so that they could see where Owl was and
Dewy and Willie both carried a saucepan and a wooden spoon.
"WAKE UP!" they shouted, and banged on the saucepans
with the wooden spoons, every time Owl's eyelids drooped.

Owl wasn't the only one they kept awake. It was impossible for ANYONE to sleep with all the shouting and crashing and banging that was going on.

"Go to sleep," cried a hundred sleepy voices.

"DON'T LISTEN TO THEM OWL!" shouted Willie.

At long last the first light of dawn crept over the horizon. And Owl was still awake.

"Thanks a lot fellows . . ." he yawned as he flew home to bed. "I couldn't have done it without your help. I'll be alright now . . . I know I will . . ."

Dewy, Basil and Willie didn't dare go to bed themselves.

"If we go to bed now and sleep all day we will be awake all night," said Basil. "Then we will be mixed up. We don't want anything like that happening to us."

They had spent the entire NIGHT keeping Owl awake, now they spent the entire DAY keeping themselves awake. They weren't the only ones yawning either. There wasn't a wide-awake animal in the wood. It seemed a very long day, but at last, it was time to go to bed. They fell asleep the instant their heads touched their pillows. They slept so soundly they didn't even wake when Owl flew over and hooted a greeting down the chimney.

"All's well in the wood," hooted Owl. "All's well."

LOST AND FOUND

Dewy was re-arranging the store cupboard. Willie was helping.

"Hand me that bag of flour next," said Dewy.

"Look out!" shouted Basil from the other side of the room. "The bo . . ." But he was too late. As Willie handed the bag across to Dewy, the bottom came undone and flour poured onto the rug like a cascading waterfall.

"Atishoo!" sneezed Willie as he was lost in the middle of a white cloud.

"Atishoo!" sneezed Dewy. HE looked like a snowbadger.

"Oh dear," said Basil. "What a mess."

When the cloud of flour settled there was a layer of white dust everywhere. Basil took charge. Dewy and Willie were sneezing too much to be able to think properly.

"Willie, you take the rug outside and get it clean," he said. "Dewy and I will clean up in here."

Willie pulled the rug out onto the grass and began to whack it with the carpet beater.

Whack! "ATISHOO!" Whack! "ATISHOO!" The harder Willie whacked the bigger the cloud got. It was half an hour before the colours on the rug showed through again.

"The rug is whacked and so am I," he sighed as he left it on the grass and went indoors to get a drink.

"Willie!" Basil was calling from the garden.
"What is it?" asked Willie, alarmed by Basil's frown.
"You didn't have to beat the rug THAT hard," said Basil accusingly. Willie gasped. There was a large bare patch right in its middle.

41

"How did that get there?" he asked.

"That's what I want to know," said Basil crossly.

"I didn't do it," said Willie. "It was alright when I left it . . . really it was." And he looked so innocent Basil had to believe him.

"Holes like that don't come by themselves," said Dewy. "I want to know where all the pieces of wool have gone."

"Perhaps the wind blew them away," said Willie.

Dewy tested for wind. "There isn't any," he said.

There wasn't a scrap of coloured wool anywhere on the grass . . . or on any of the bushes . . . or anywhere else.

"Very odd," said Basil, scratching his head. "Very odd indeed. I don't understand this at all."

There was a polite cough behind them.

"Er . . . does this belong to you?" asked a voice. They turned and saw a very embarrassed-looking dormouse. She was struggling with a large bundle of loose woollen pieces.

"They're from OUR rug," said Willie indignantly. "What are YOU doing with them?"

"I think you'd better explain," said Basil sternly.

The dormouse sighed.
"It's getting close to the time
when we dormice settle down for
our winter sleep," she said.
"The children were only trying
to help. When they saw the
rug they thought how snug it
would keep us through the
winter, so they helped
themselves to a little piece
of it."

"A little piece . . ."
sniffed Willie. "That doesn't
look like a little piece to me."

"There's some more of it
at home," sighed the dormouse.
"I couldn't carry it all. You
had better come and get it."

But when they arrived at
the dormouse home they found
the dormice children already
curled up and asleep in a
rainbow-coloured bed.

"They didn't waste any
time, did they?" said Willie.

They looked so cosy and
warm Dewy would not let their
mother wake them.

43

"Let them sleep on," he said.

"But what about your rug?" said the dormouse.

"We'll find something to mend it with," said Basil. "Don't you worry any more." And that is why one of the rugs in Ash Lodge has a brown middle and rainbow-coloured borders.

BEGINNERS PLEASE

The weather was getting colder. Much colder. One
morning, there was a thick white frost covering everything
in icy lace.

"Come out here and take a look," called Basil.

"Ow!" cried Willie as he slipped on an icy patch.

Basil helped him to his feet.

"I should try to go round the icy patches if I were you," he said.

The ducks came waddling across from the pond. They looked very unhappy.

"Isn't it slippery?" said Willie cheerfully.

"You don't have to tell US that," they quacked crossly. "We know already . . . we've all got bruises to prove it."

"Oh . . ." said Willie. "Did you slip too?"

"Slip . . . slip . . ." they quacked. "We've done nothing else but slip." One of them held out a webbed foot. "See that . . . that's for swimming with . . . not for sliding on . . ."

"Then why don't you swim with it?" Willie was puzzled.

"Can't swim without water."

Willie laughed. "You've got a pond full of water."

"That's what you think," quacked the ducks. "Just take a look at the pond."

So they did. It was covered from bank to bank with a thick layer of ice. There wasn't enough water for a duck to get a foot in, let alone sit down and swim.

"What's to be done?" asked the ducks.

"I'll show you what's to be done," said Basil. He
went to the shed and came back with a wooden mallet.

CRASH went the mallet onto the edge of the ice. The
ice cracked. CRASH went the mallet again. The ice
splintered and broke. Basil chipped away at the broken
edge until there was a hole big enough for the ducks to
swim in.

"Quack . . ." they said. "Thanks very much Basil. Oh
what a relief it is to get our feet back into the water."
And they paddled round and round quacking happily, not
caring a jot how cold the water was.

Basil picked up a piece of the broken ice.

"It's very thick," he said.

"Thick enough for US to slide on?" asked Dewy hopefully.

"I'm sure it is," said Basil and stepped onto the pond.

"Basil . . . DON'T!" Willie covered his eyes and waited for the splash. It didn't come.

Swish . . . sh . . . sh . . . went Basil across the ice.

Swish . . . sh . . . sh . . . went Dewy after him.

"You'll never get ME on there," said Willie. But
Basil and Dewy seemed to be having such a good time he said
he would give it a try if they promised to help him.

"Hold me," he said. "Don't let me fall." They held
him SO tightly he couldn't have fallen if he had wanted to.

"Try it on your own now,"
said Basil, when Willie had
had a few practise slides.
"Wheeee!" cried Willie.
"OOOOH!" cried Willie as he
wobbled. "OWWWW!" cried
Willie as he fell.
"You're supposed to stay
on your feet," laughed Dewy
as Willie slid across the pond
on his tail.
"I know I am . . ." grumbled
Willie. "I suppose you
think I did that on purpose."
Basil and Dewy helped him
to his feet.
"Try again . . ." they said.
"I don't want to," said
Willie. But they gave him a
gentle push and this time he managed to stay on his feet.
"I can do it . . . I can do it . . ." he cried. Now he knew
he COULD slide, he practised and practised, and though he
fell over dozens of times he really began to get rather good.
"You're cleverer than you think," said Dewy.
"You mean I'm cleverer than YOU think," said Willie.